For Flora,
who is all kinds
of special
—T. S.

To all kinds of
special family
and friends.
—F. M.

SIMON & SCHUSTER BOOKS FOR YOUNG READERS

An imprint of Simon & Schuster Children's Publishing Division

1230 Avenue of the Americas, New York, New York 10020

Text © 2023 by Tammi Sauer

Illustration © 2023 by Fernando Martin

Book design by Lizzy Bromley © 2023 by Simon & Schuster, Inc.

All rights reserved, including the right of reproduction in whole or in part in any form.

SIMON & SCHUSTER BOOKS FOR YOUNG READERS and related marks are trademarks of Simon & Schuster, Inc.

For information about special discounts for bulk purchases, please contact Simon & Schuster Special Sales

at 1-866-506-1949 or business@simonandschuster.com.

The Simon & Schuster Speakers Bureau can bring authors to your live event. For more information or to book an event,

contact the Simon & Schuster Speakers Bureau at 1-866-248-3049 or visit our website at www.simonspeakers.com.

The text for this book was set in Colby.

The illustrations for this book were rendered digitally.

Manufactured in China · 0123 SCP · First Edition

2 4 6 8 10 9 7 5 3 1

Library of Congress Cataloging-in-Publication Data

Names: Sauer, Tammi, author. | Martin, Fernando, (Illustrator), illustrator.

Title: All kinds of special / Tammi Sauer ; illustrated by Fernando Martin.

Description: New York : Simon & Schuster Books for Young Readers, 2023. |

Audience: Ages 4–8. | Audience: Grades 2–3. | Summary: Mia discovers the

joy of community and friendship when she and Mama share the delicious

fruit from their mango tree with their new neighbors.

Identifiers: LCCN 2021060680 (print) | LCCN 2021060681 (ebook)

| ISBN 9781534496033 (hardcover) | ISBN 9781534496040 (ebook)

Subjects: CYAC: Mango—Fiction. | Trees—Fiction. | Sharing—Fiction. |

Neighborliness—Fiction. | LCGFT: Picture books.

Classification: LCC PZ7.S2502 Al 2023 (print) | LCC PZ7.S2502 (ebook)

| DDC [E]—dc23

LC record available at https://lccn.loc.gov/2021060680

LC ebook record available at https://lccn.loc.gov/2021060681

# ALL KINDS OF SPECIAL

Written by Tammi Sauer
Illustrated by Fernando Martin

A Paula Wiseman Book
Simon & Schuster Books for Young Readers
New York  London  Toronto  Sydney  New Delhi

# I'M MIA.
This is Mama.
And this is our
new favorite fact.
We have a house.

A house!
Five rooms.
Eleven windows.
And a whole lot
of promise.

Our apartment was
all kinds of special.

One good-bye
was *extra* hard.

But a house has been Mama's dream for so long,
it couldn't help but grow into my dream too.
And this house?
It comes with a yard *and* a mango tree.

This place is our own
personal queendom.

Each morning, I prop my elbows onto
my windowsill and watch for mangos.
Nothing looks close to ready.
I'm about to think I'll never find one
that's ripe.

Then *I do!*

I hurry outside.
And I give that mango a tug.
Mama joins me in the yard, and I tell
her my new favorite fact.
"Our tree made a mango!"

Don't get me wrong. We've had mangos before.
But this isn't just *any* mango. This one's ours.
Mama pops that mango into a brown paper bag.

We have extra waiting to do because our
mango has an extra round of ripening to do.

Finally-finally-*finally*, it's ready.

My knee won't stop bouncing as
Mama prepares our mango.
She hands a slice to me.

And that first bite?
It tastes, smells, looks, and feels like
summer all at the exact same time!

The next day I go to my spot at the window.

More mangos.

The day after that,

even more

mangos.

And the day after that?
**Well, take a look.**

Soon Mama and I know just about every mango recipe there is.
Even so, we have a situation on our hands.
It's called **TOO MANY MANGOS.**

Side by side, we study our tree.
"Any ideas?" Mama asks because she's
always nudging me to think some up.
I keep on staring at our tree.

Then I step back and open my eyes to our entire block.
And that's when I get my idea. "Something this good
ought to be shared."

Mama smiles and says, "You know,
that's my new favorite fact."

Before long, our house with its five rooms, eleven windows, and a whole lot of promise is the busiest, chattiest spot in the neighborhood. And I know—just *know*—

this is the start of **all kinds of special.**
One of our neighbors is practically an expert
with the fruit picker.

One shares a recipe that is brand-new to Mama.

And another makes me think
our mango tree is about to grow
something *extra* sweet.

I breathe it all in and have myself a new favorite fact.
**There's no such thing as too many mangos.**